MARVEL

GUARDIANS OF THE GALAXY VOL. 2

GUARDIANS

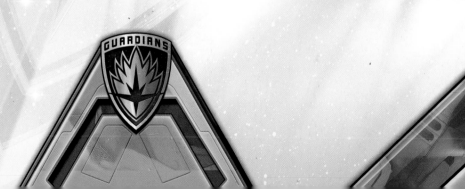

marvelkids.com

© 2017 MARVEL.

Illustrations by Ron Lim, Andy Smith, Andy Troy, and Chris Sotomayor

Cover design by Elaine Lopez-Levine. Cover illustration by Ron Lim, Andy Smith, Andy Troy, and Chris Sotomayor

Little, Brown and Company
Hachette Book Group
1290 Avenue of the Americas, New York, NY 10104
Visit us at lb-kids.com
marvelkids.com

First Edition: April 2017

Little, Brown and Company is a division of Hachette Book Group, Inc.
The Little, Brown name and logo are trademarks of Hachette Book Group, Inc.

The publisher is not responsible for websites (or their content) that are not owned by the publisher.

ISBNs: 978-0-316-27162-2 (pbk.), 978-0-316-55386-5 (ebook), 978-0-316-55387-2 (ebook), 978-0-316-31418-3 (ebook)

Printed in the United States of America

CW

10 9 8 7 6 5 4 3 2

MARVEL

GUARDIANS OF THE GALAXY VOL. 2

THE RETURN OF ROCKET AND GROOT

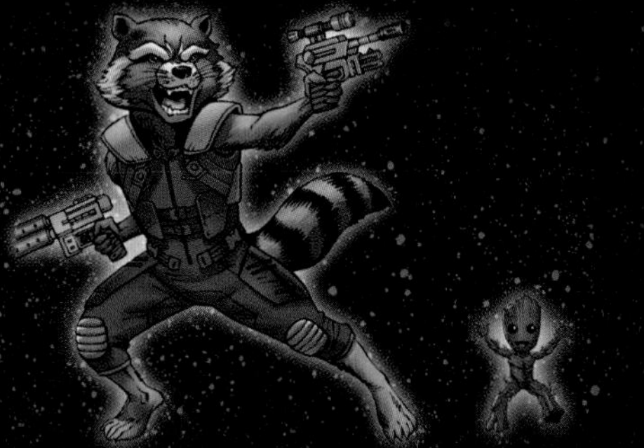

Adapted by Charles Cho

Illustrations by Ron Lim, Andy Smith, Andy Troy, and Chris Sotomayor

Based on the Major Motion Picture

Produced by Kevin Feige, p.g.a.

Written and Directed by James Gunn

LB

LITTLE, BROWN AND COMPANY

New York Boston

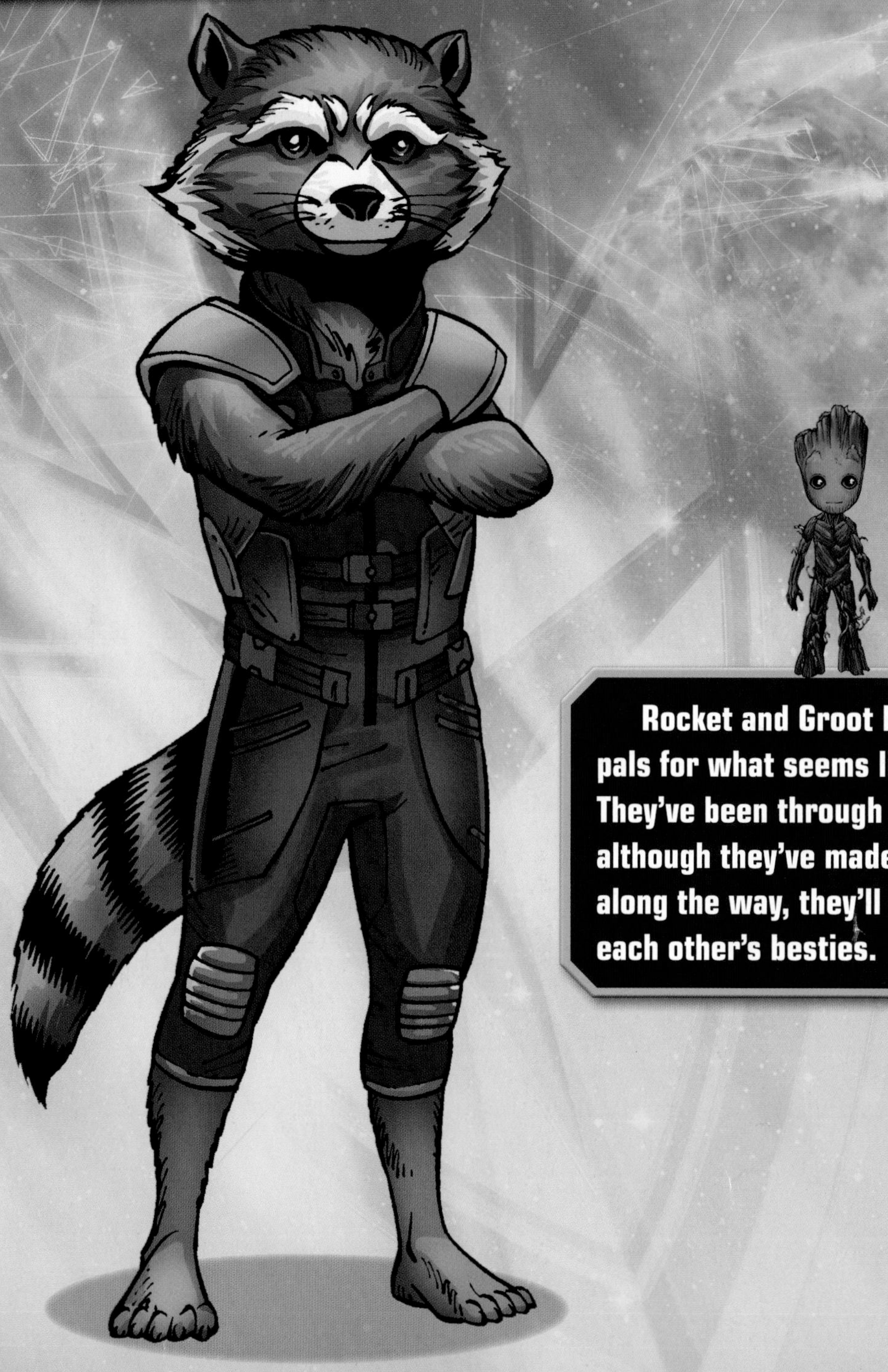

Rocket and Groot have been pals for what seems like forever! They've been through a lot, and although they've made new friends along the way, they'll always be each other's besties.

Not too long ago, they became part of the Guardians of the Galaxy, a group of intergalactic adventurers. Peter Quill (also known as Star-Lord), Gamora, and Drax don't always follow the rules, but they do always fight for what is right. Sometimes Rocket gets ideas of his own, but thankfully, Groot is usually there to keep him in check, reminding him, "I am Groot!"

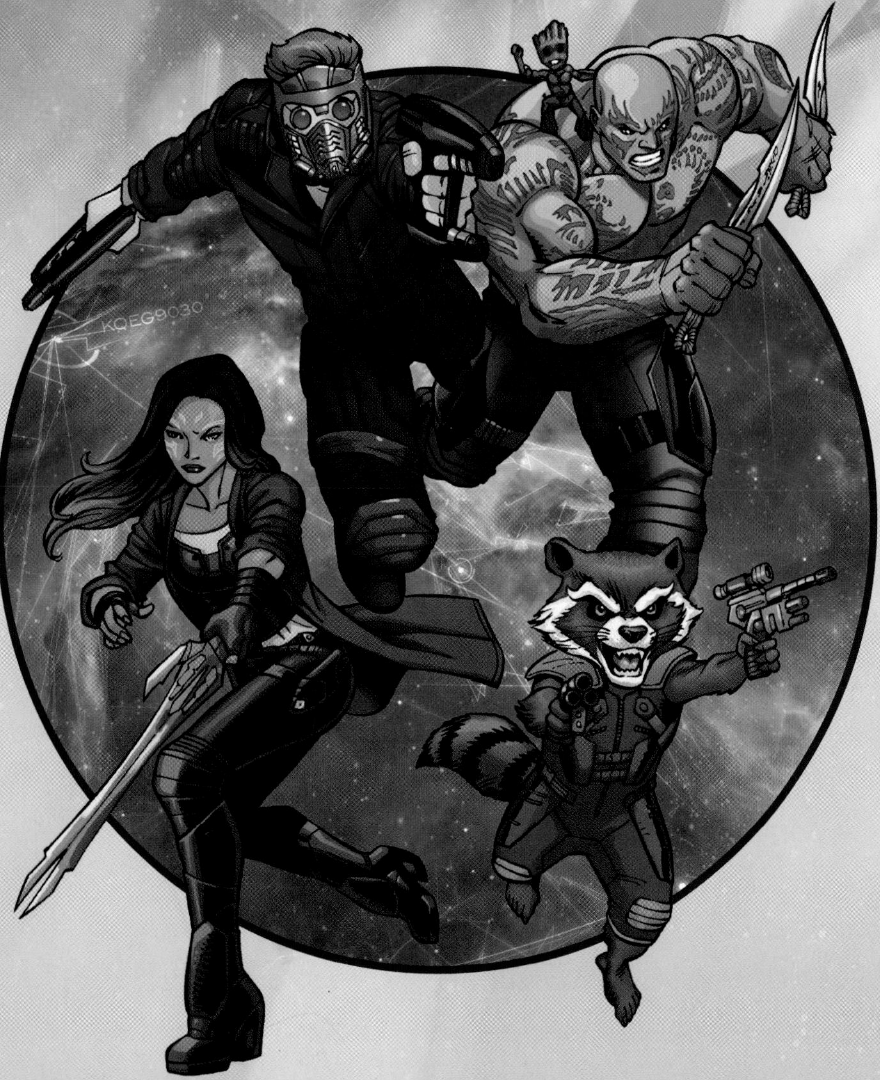
KQEG9030

Today, the Guardians are preparing for a battle. They've been hired by inhabitants of the Sovereign—a magnificent, golden planet—to protect six conductor towers. Since the towers hold batteries that are some of the most sought-after energy sources in the galaxy, the Guardians must be ready for anything.

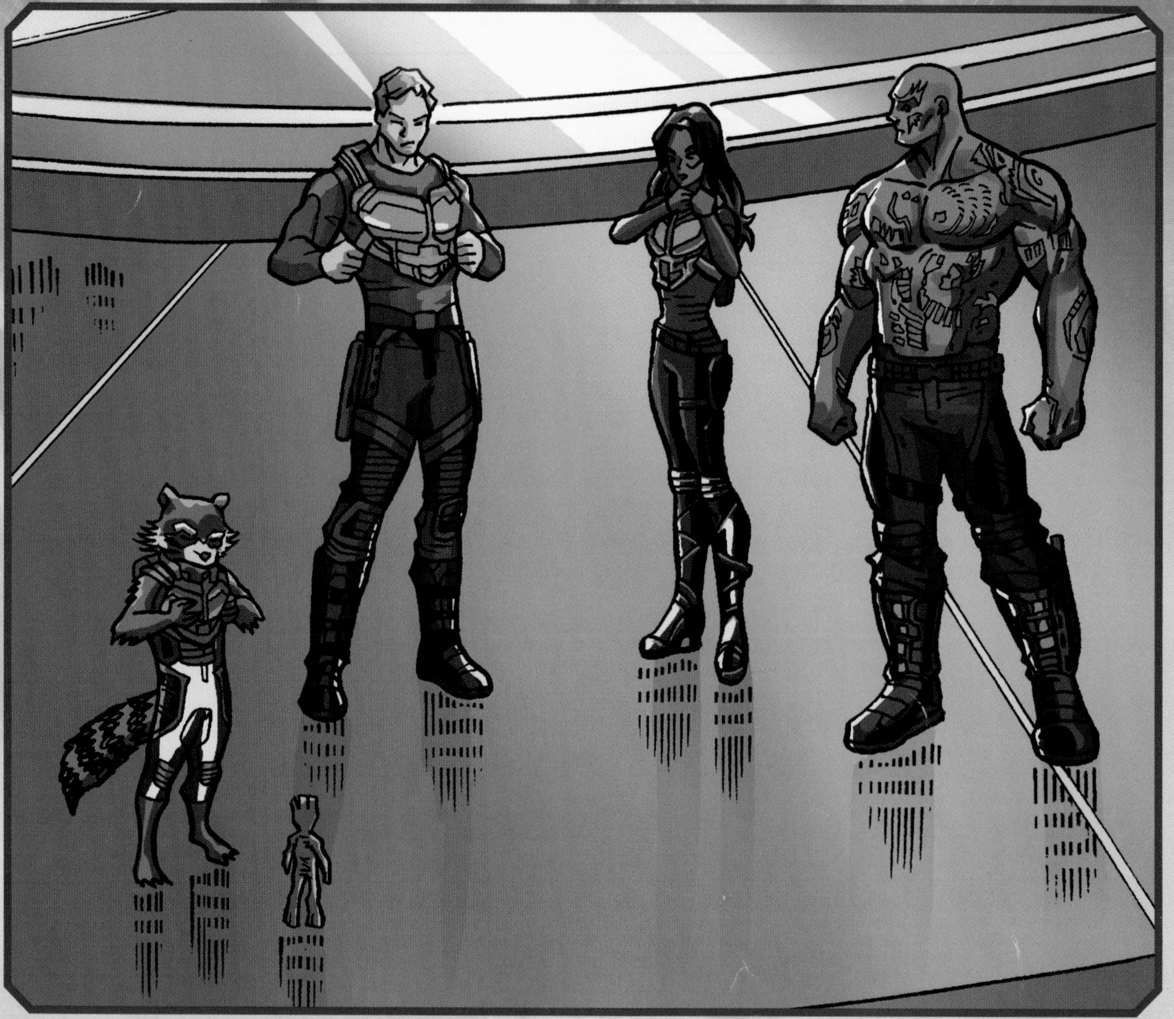

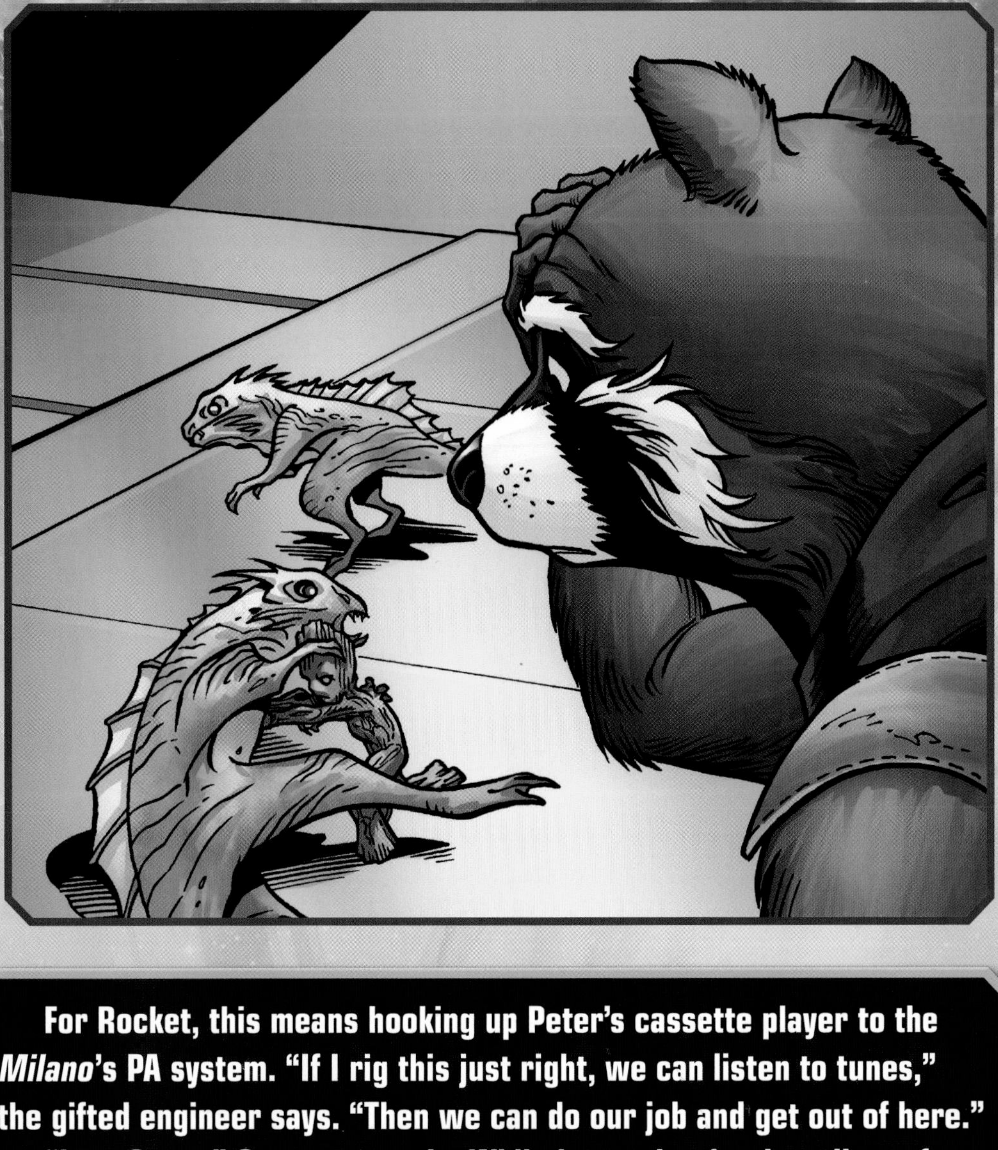

For Rocket, this means hooking up Peter's cassette player to the *Milano*'s PA system. "If I rig this just right, we can listen to tunes," the gifted engineer says. "Then we can do our job and get out of here."

"I am Groot," Groot responds. While he used to be the tallest of the Guardians, an accident made the treelike creature a fraction of his former size. Now he helps out however he can, whether it's yelling helpful reminders to Rocket, or tussling with Orlani.

Suddenly, a massive inter-dimensional crack appears. It's time for the Guardians of the Galaxy to take their fighting stances.

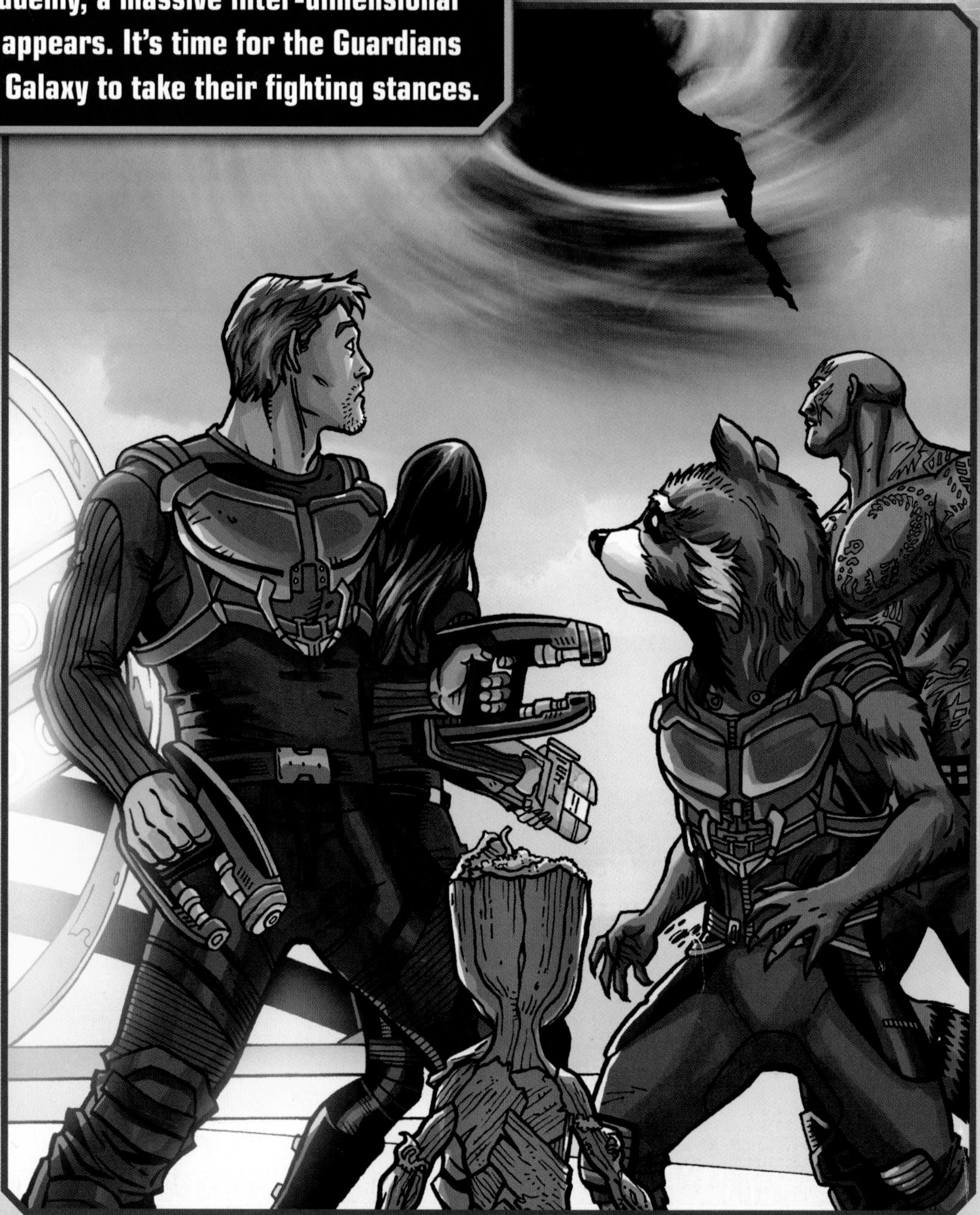

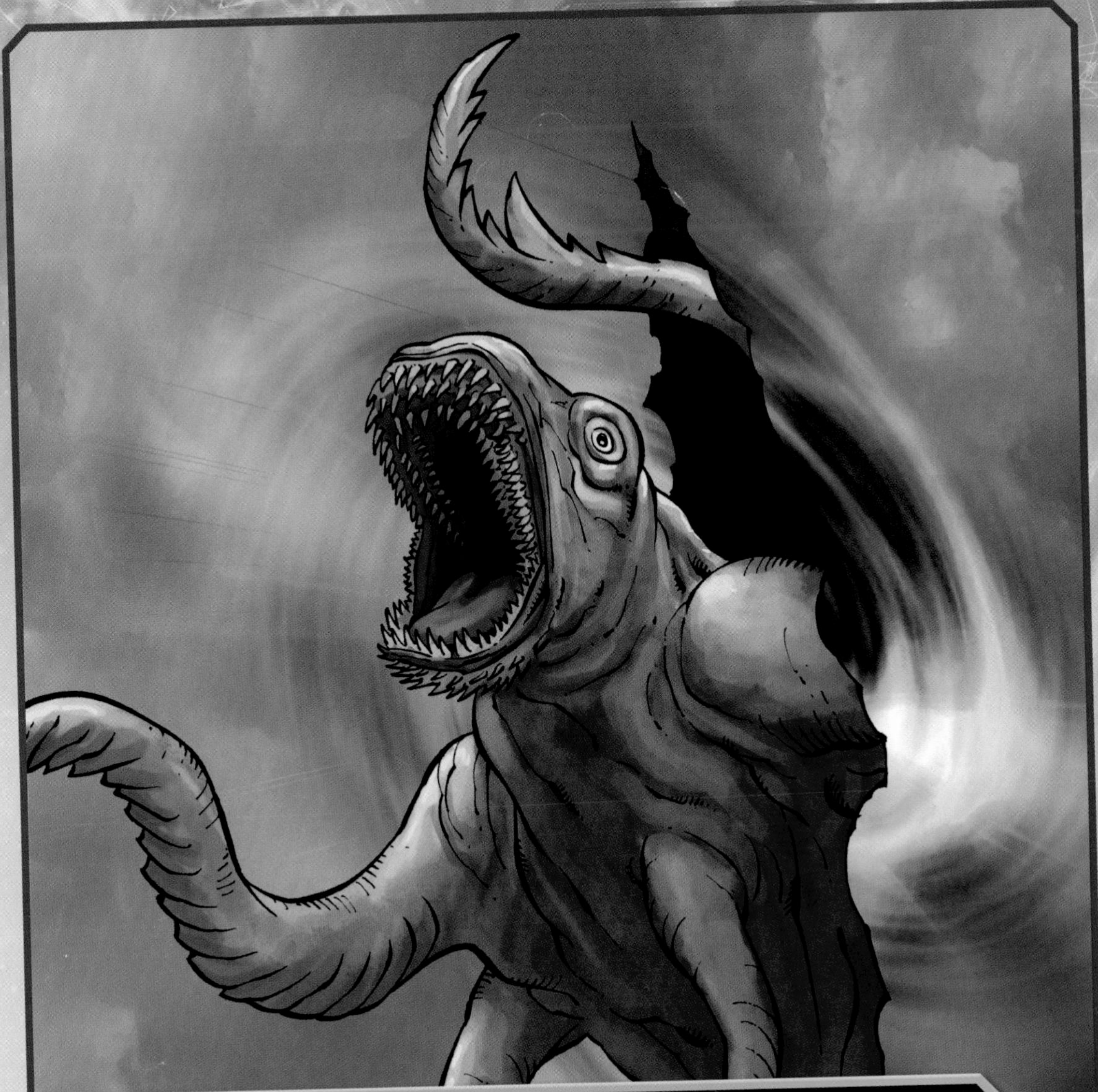

The gigantic, pale-pink Abilisk that emerges is like nothing the team has seen before. Colorful waves pulse from its mouth, distorting the space around it. Keeping a giant, battery-hungry space worm from its food is not going to be easy!

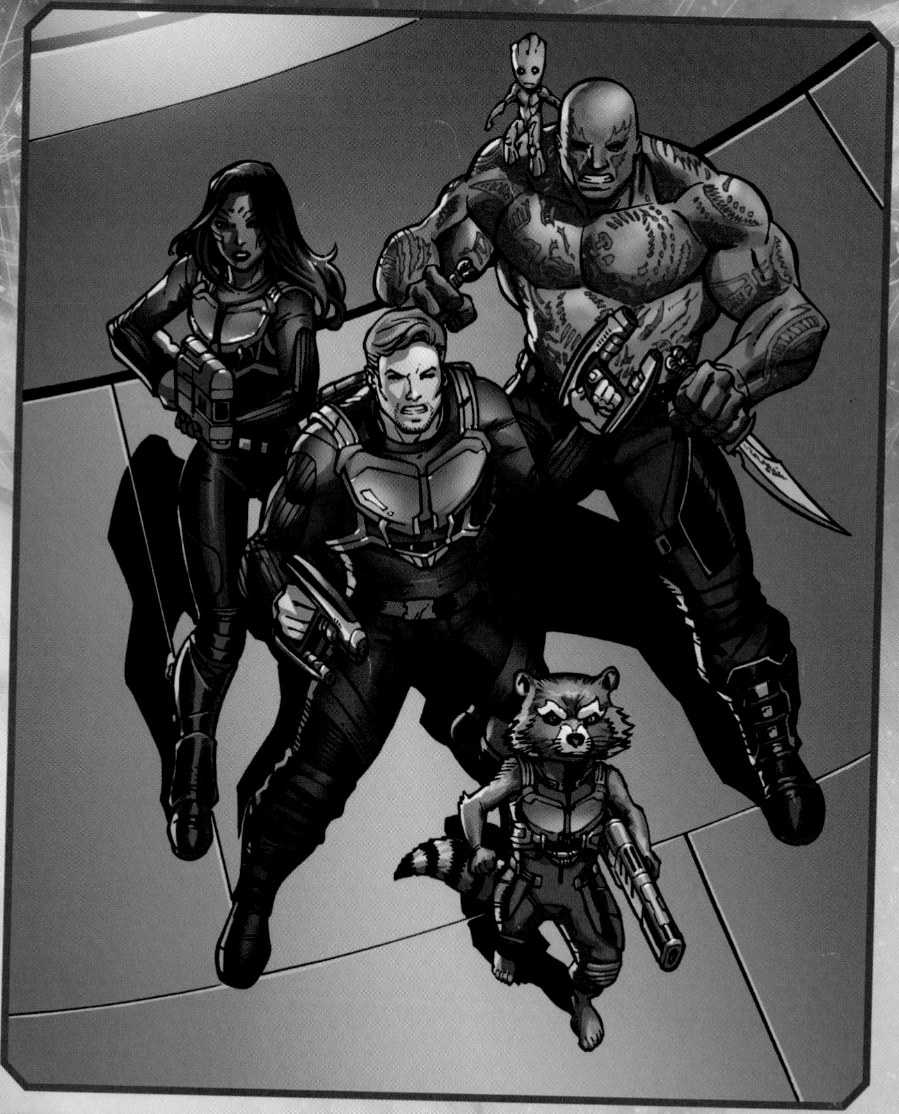

But the Guardians have something the beast does not: music! Rocket presses a button, blasting Awesome Mix Tape Vol. 2 and pumping up the entire team, especially Peter. The Guardians are ready for a fight!

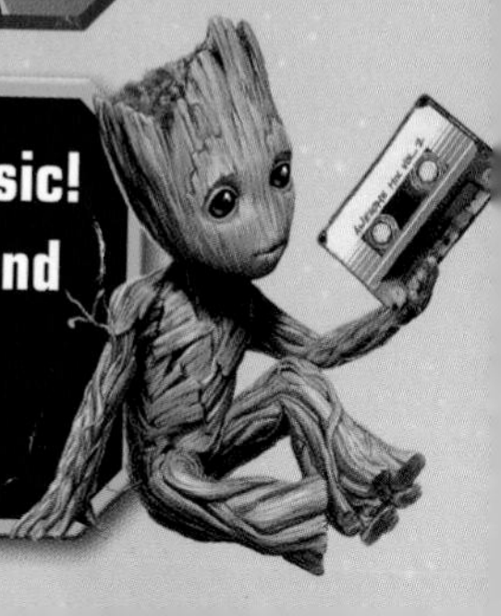

Peter turns to his friends and says, “We’ve got this!” He reaches up, turns on his mask, and leads the charge. Rocket, Peter, and Gamora use their space rigs to move into position.

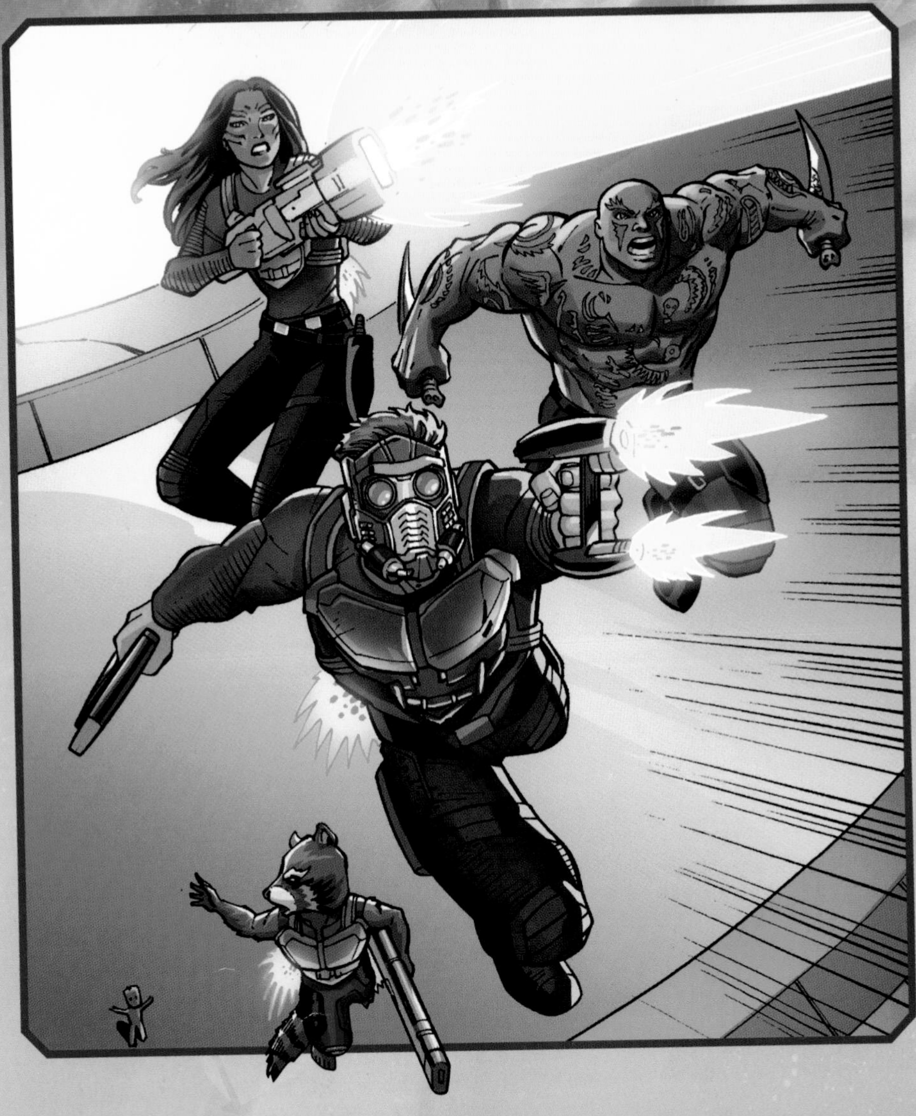

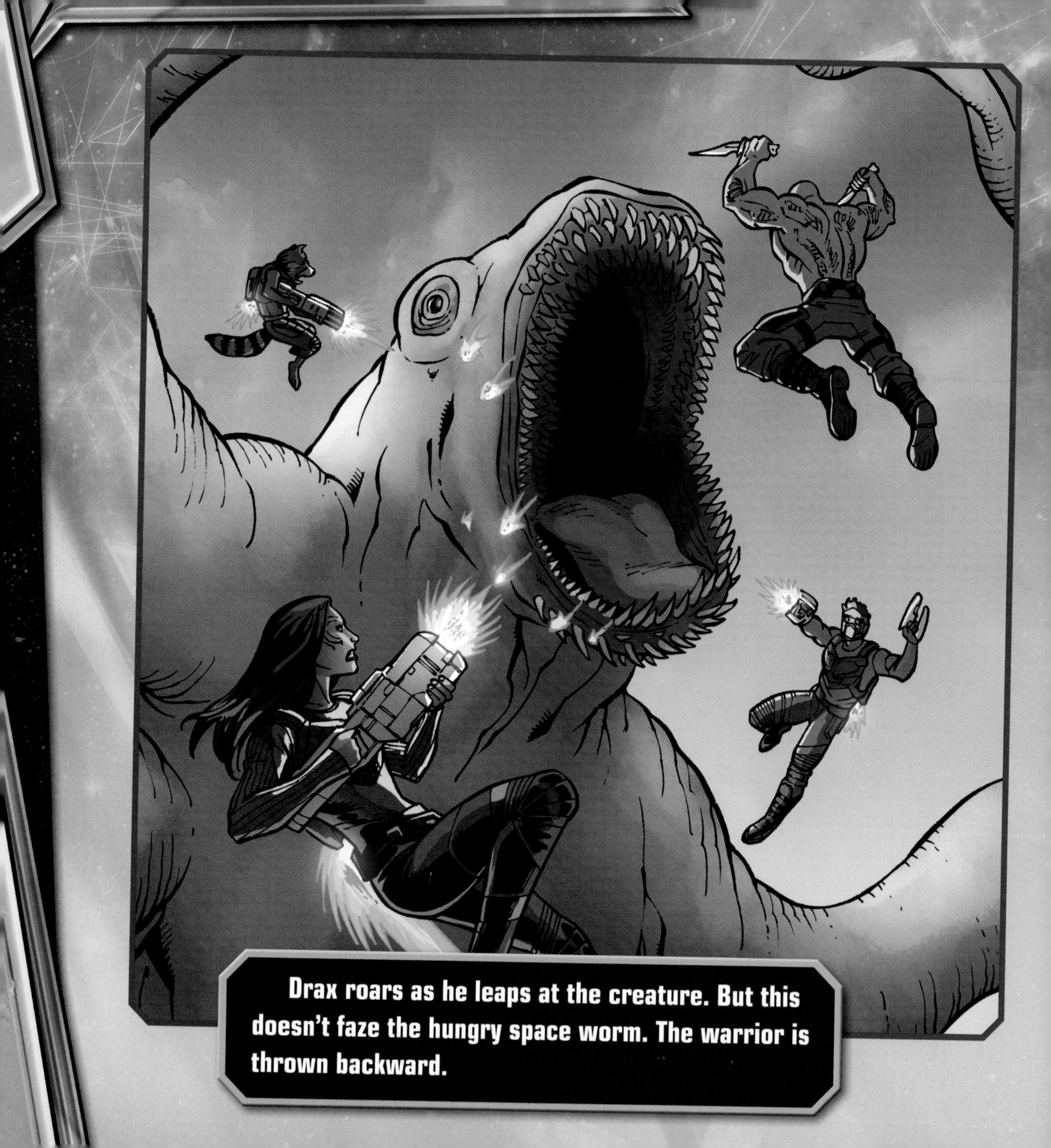

Drax roars as he leaps at the creature. But this doesn't faze the hungry space worm. The warrior is thrown backward.

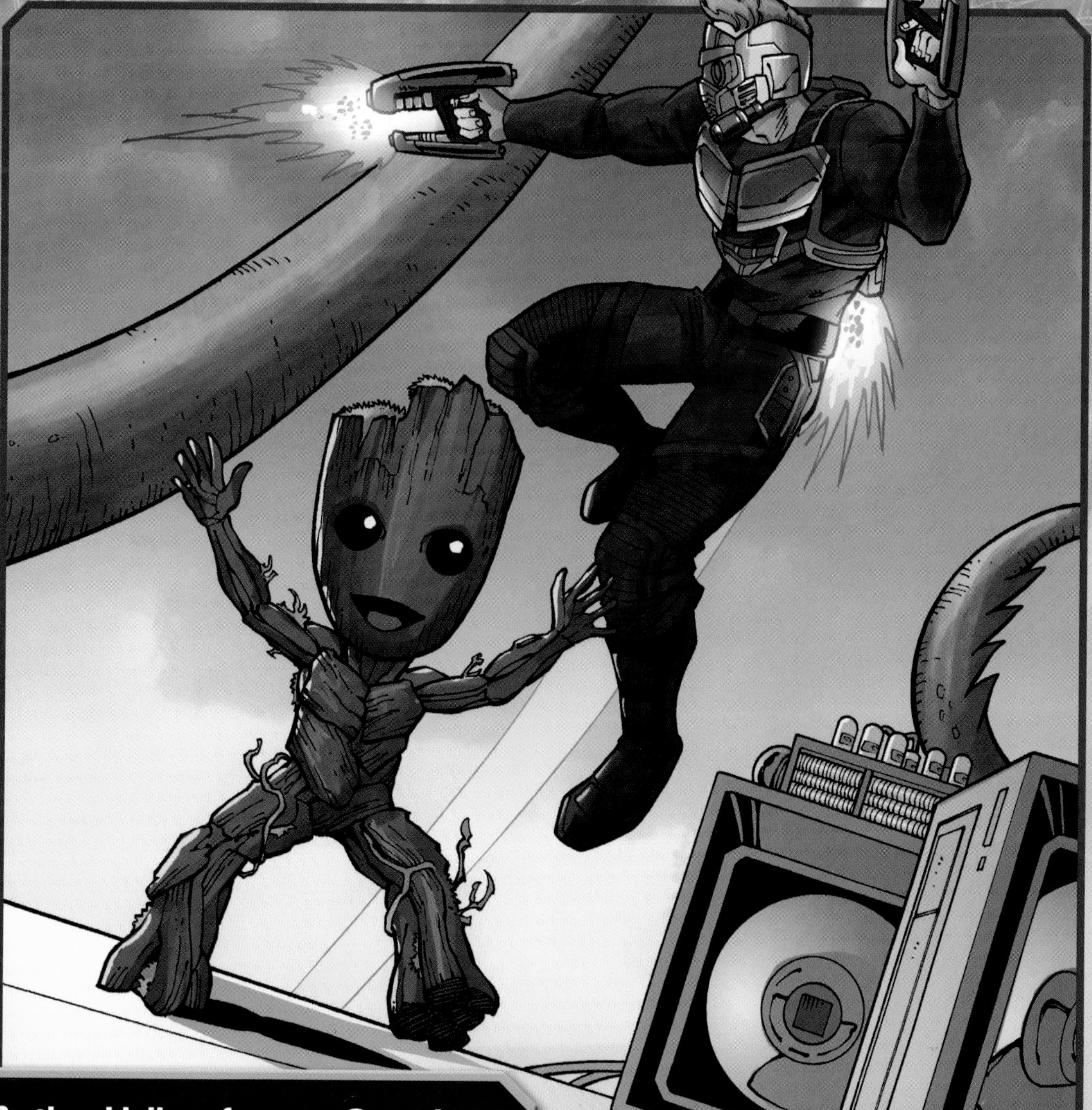

On the sidelines for now, Groot jams to the music and cheers. "I am Groot!" he encourages.

Just then Peter notices the Abilisk has been wounded. "Gamora—there! On the neck!" he yells.

"I see it," Gamora responds coolly. "Get its attention. I'll take care of the rest." Peter and Rocket jet upward and try to distract the creature. Without a second thought, Gamora finishes the battle once and for all.

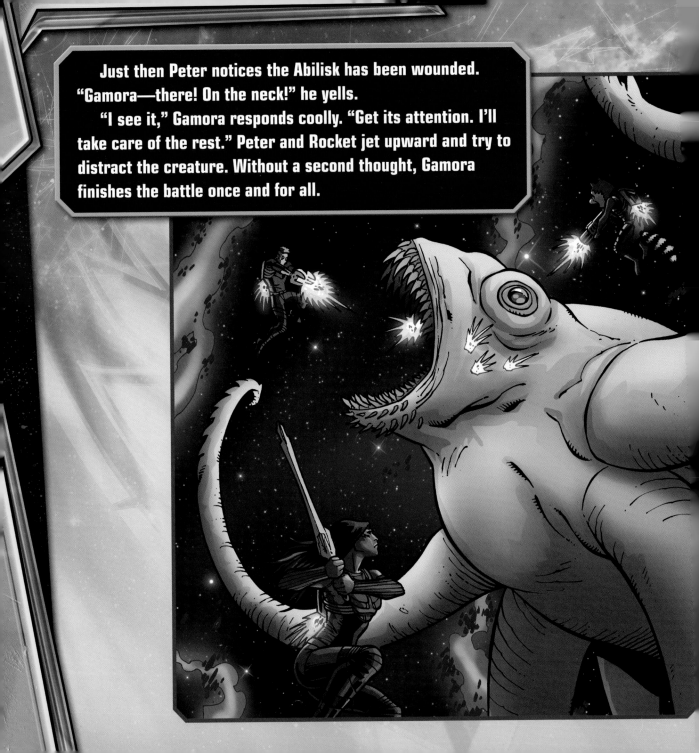

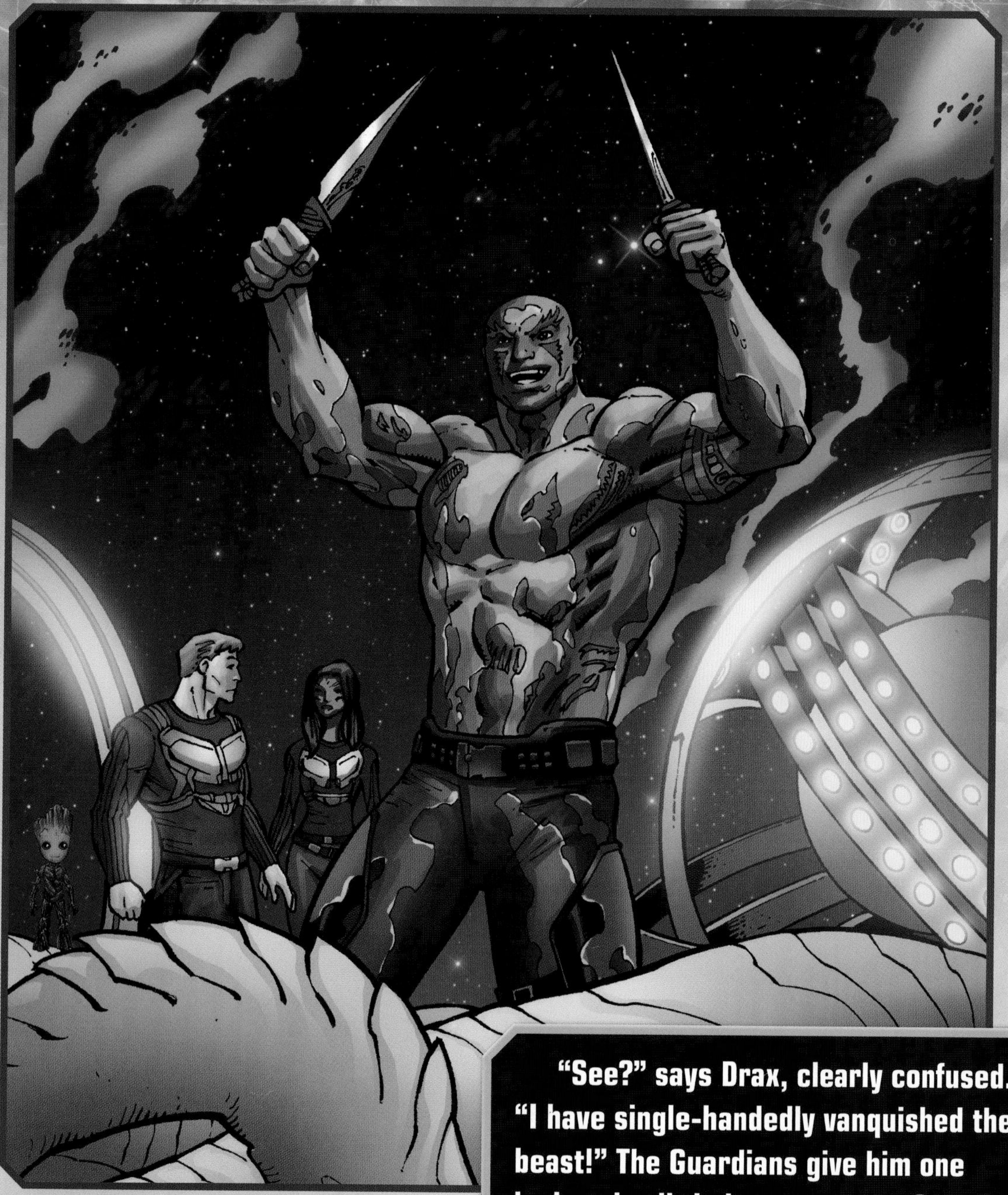

"See?" says Drax, clearly confused. "I have single-handedly vanquished the beast!" The Guardians give him one look and roll their eyes—even Groot!

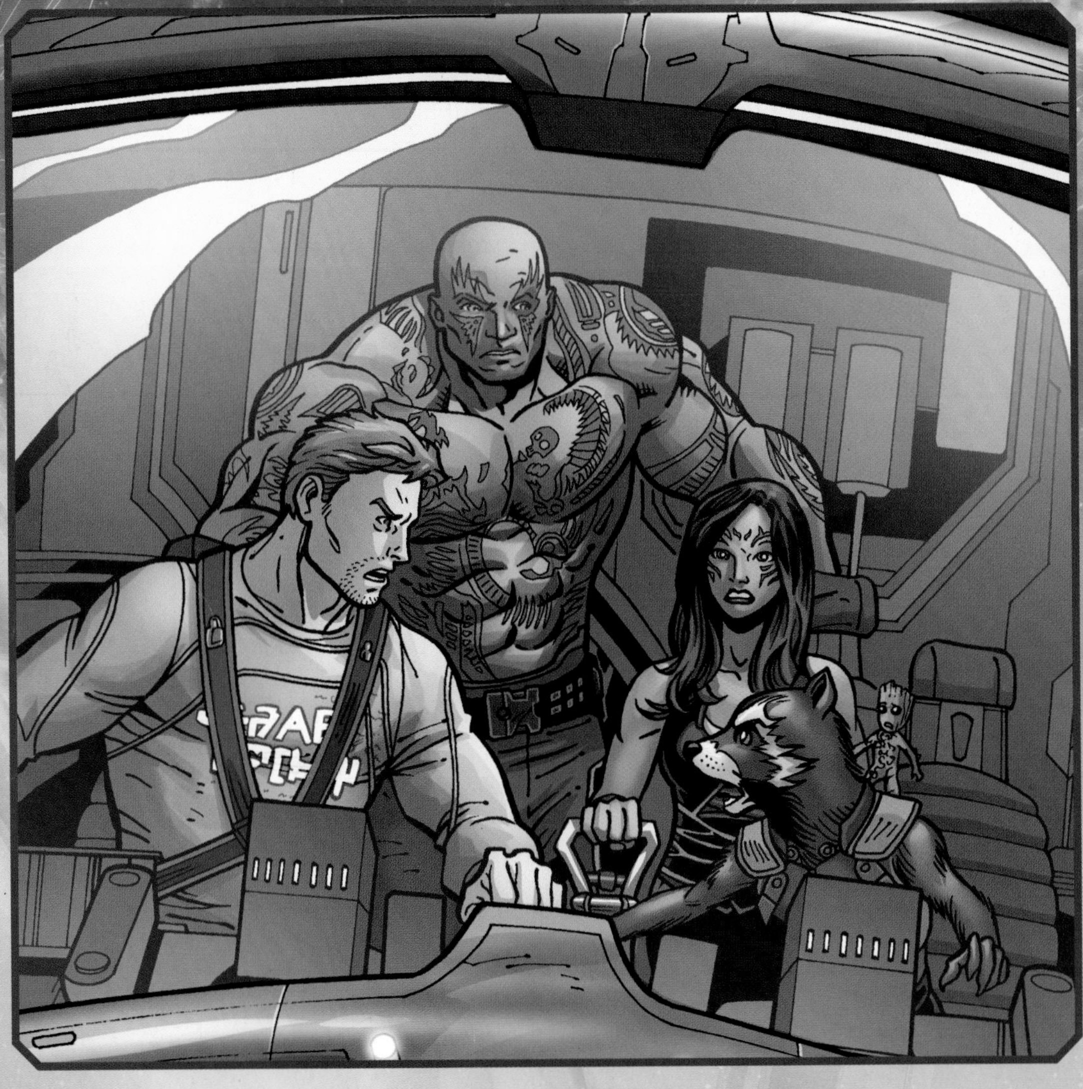

Soon after, the motley crew of heroes goes to claim their reward from the Sovereign. Peter reminds the Guardians to be on their best behavior—especially Rocket, who doesn't seem to have an interest in manners.

"I am Groot," Groot reminds his best friend.

When they enter the main chamber of the high priestess Ayesha, the woman looks down at the Guardians from her throne with a smirk. Gamora is not impressed. "Your people promised something in trade for our services. Bring it and we shall gladly be on our way."

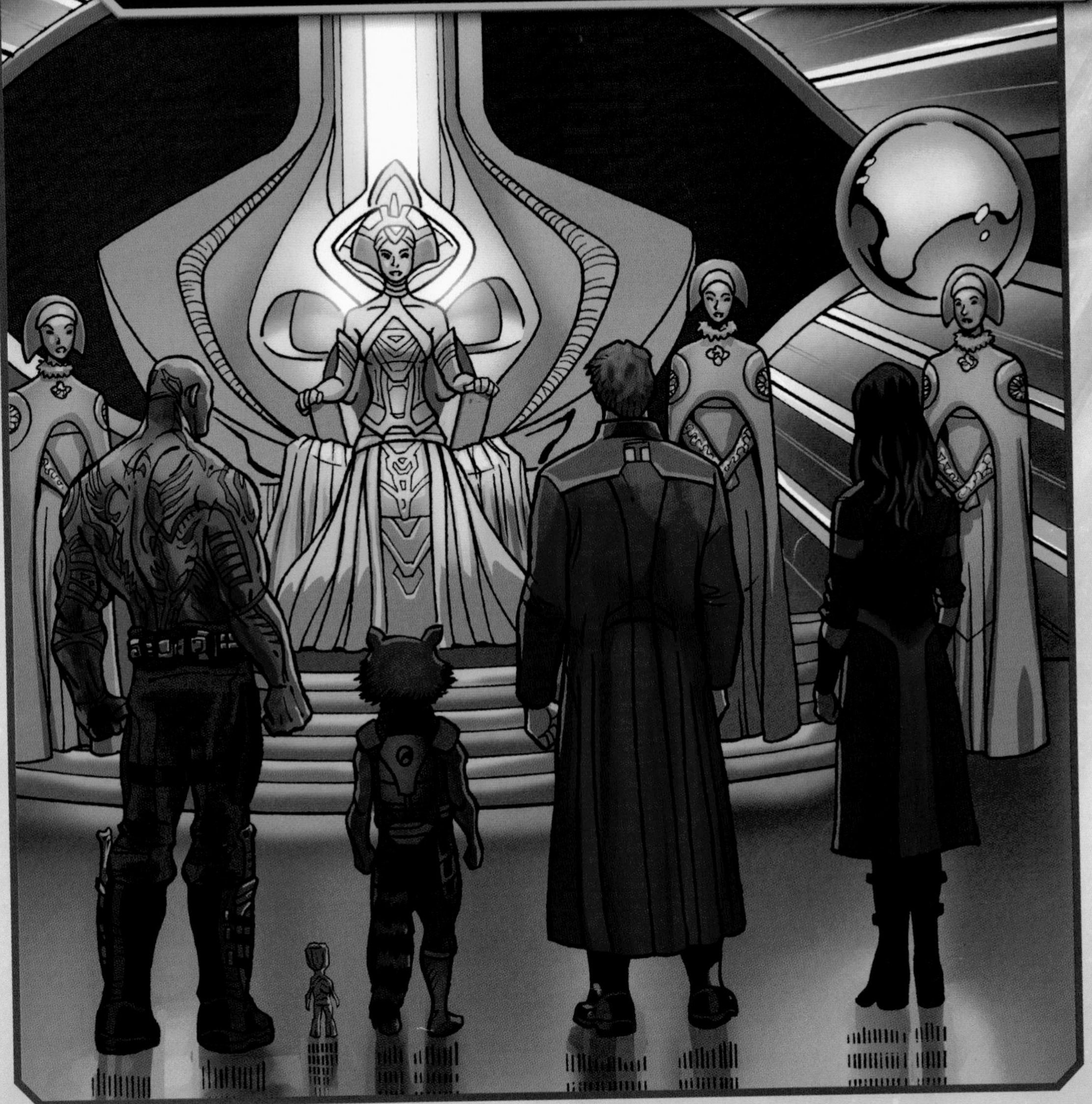

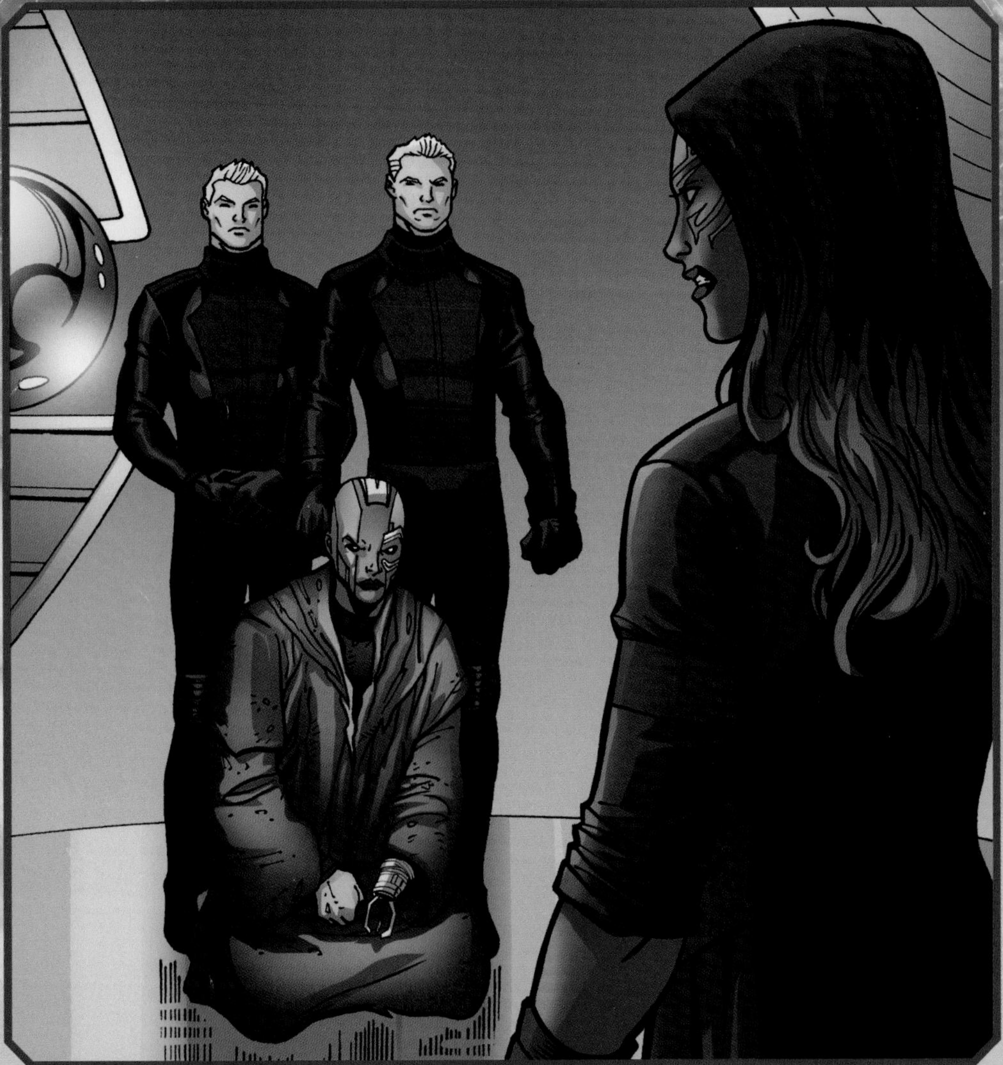

Ayesha nods and two guards return with the Guardians' reward: Gamora's adopted sister, Nebula. The women have fought for as long as they can remember and neither is excited to see the other. "Family reunion! *Yay!*" Peter says, trying to lighten the mood.

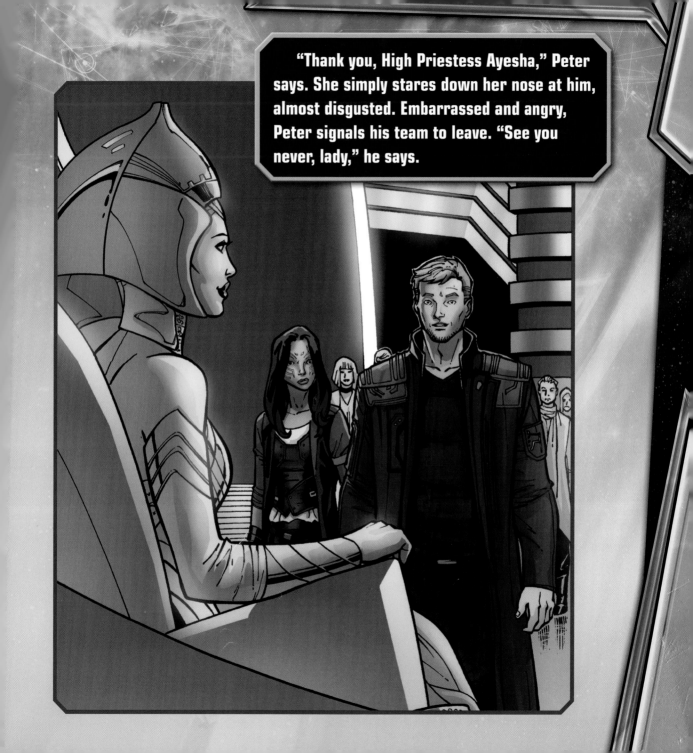

"Thank you, High Priestess Ayesha," Peter says. She simply stares down her nose at him, almost disgusted. Embarrassed and angry, Peter signals his team to leave. "See you never, lady," he says.

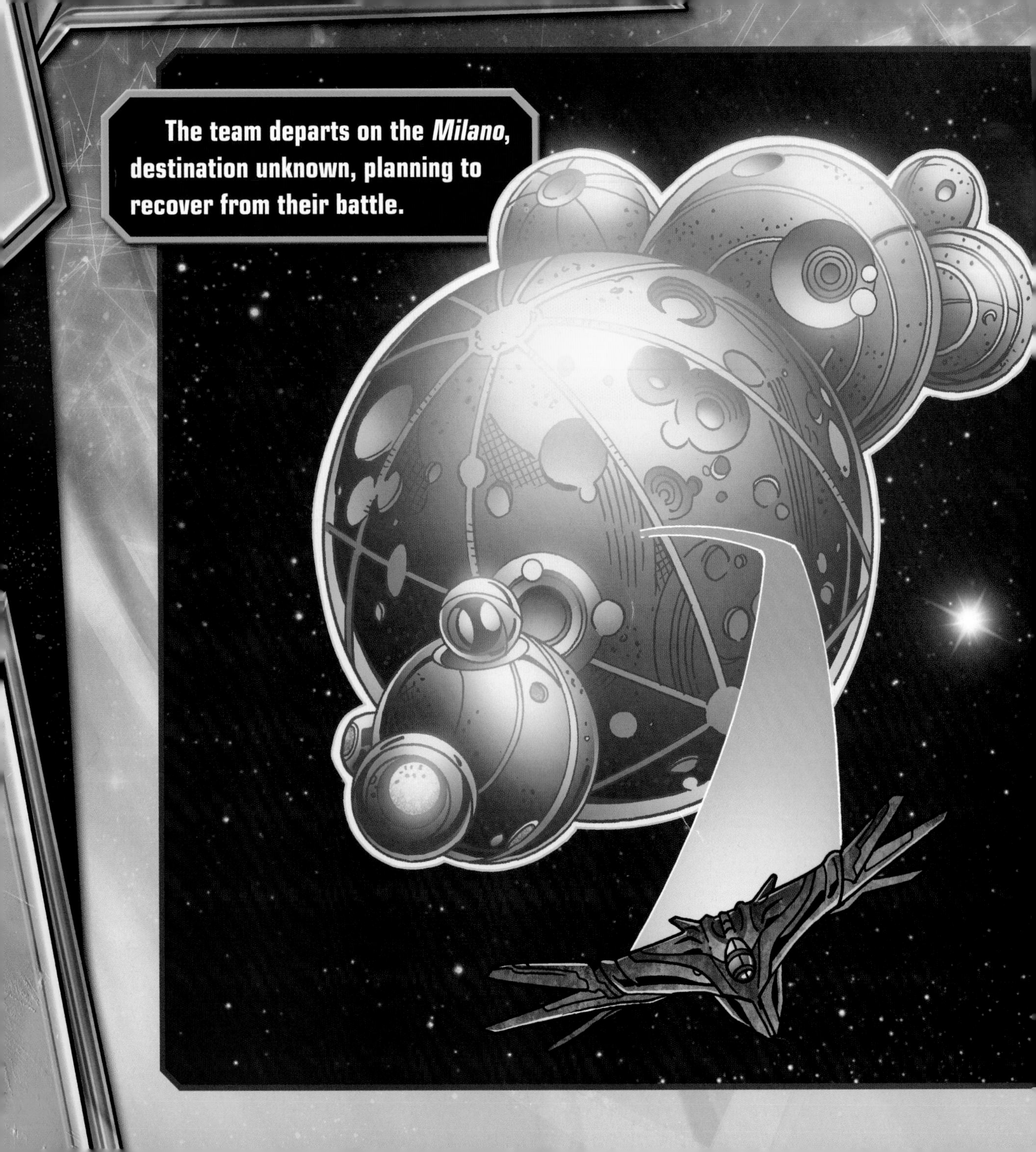
The team departs on the *Milano*, destination unknown, planning to recover from their battle.

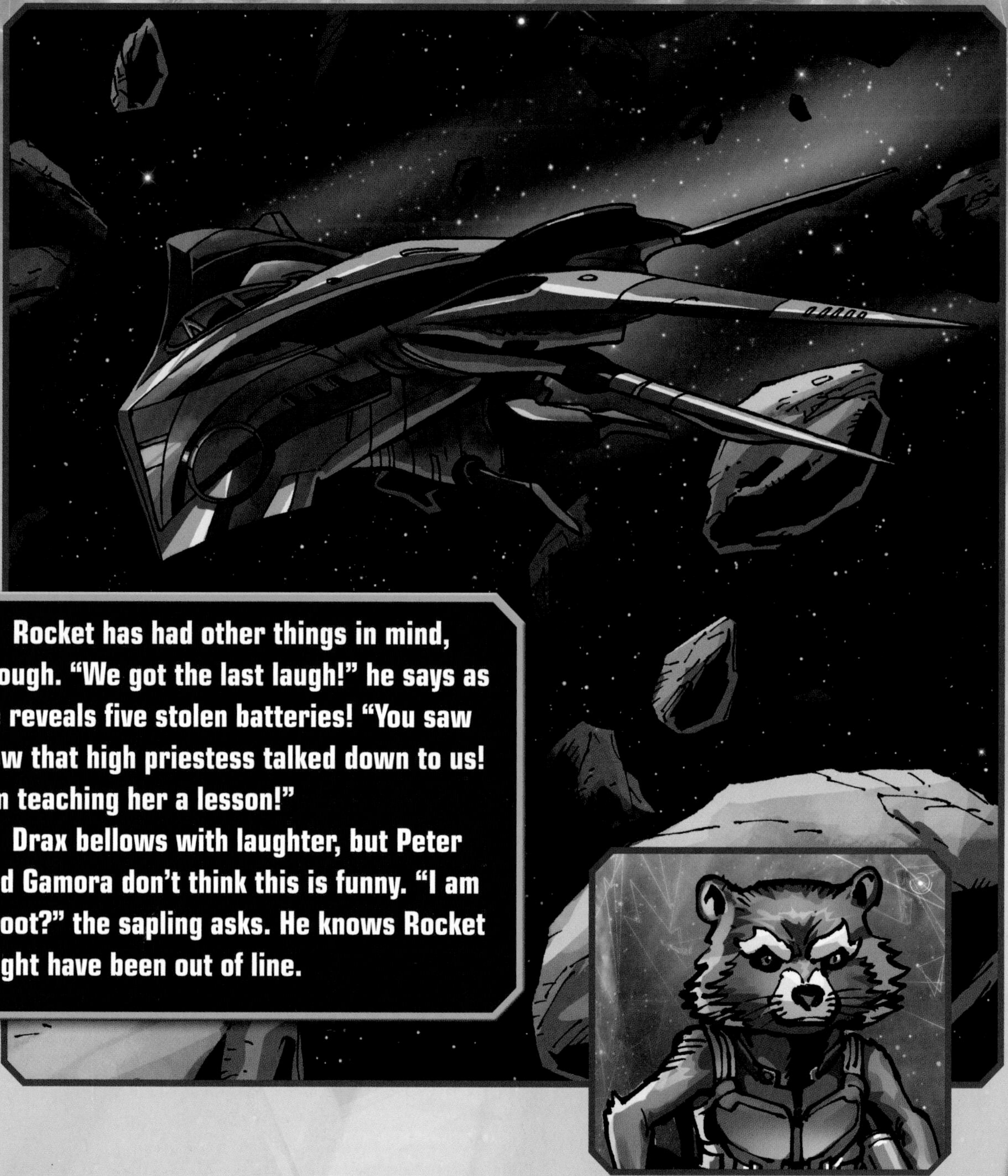

Rocket has had other things in mind, though. "We got the last laugh!" he says as he reveals five stolen batteries! "You saw how that high priestess talked down to us! I'm teaching her a lesson!"

Drax bellows with laughter, but Peter and Gamora don't think this is funny. "I am Groot?" the sapling asks. He knows Rocket might have been out of line.

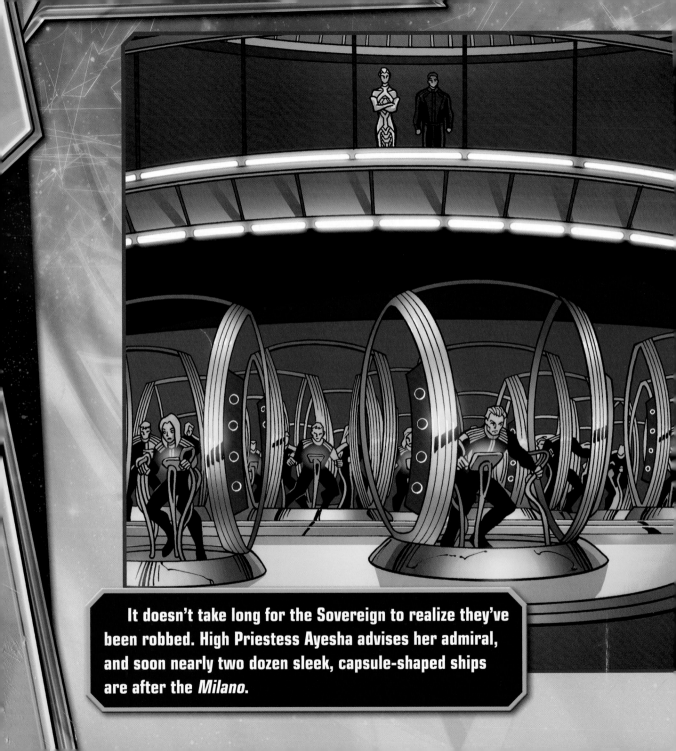

It doesn't take long for the Sovereign to realize they've been robbed. High Priestess Ayesha advises her admiral, and soon nearly two dozen sleek, capsule-shaped ships are after the *Milano*.

Just like their pilots, the omnicraft are fast and precise, but the Guardians have heart. Playing more music, Rocket and Peter argue over who should do the flying.

"I am Groot," says Groot.

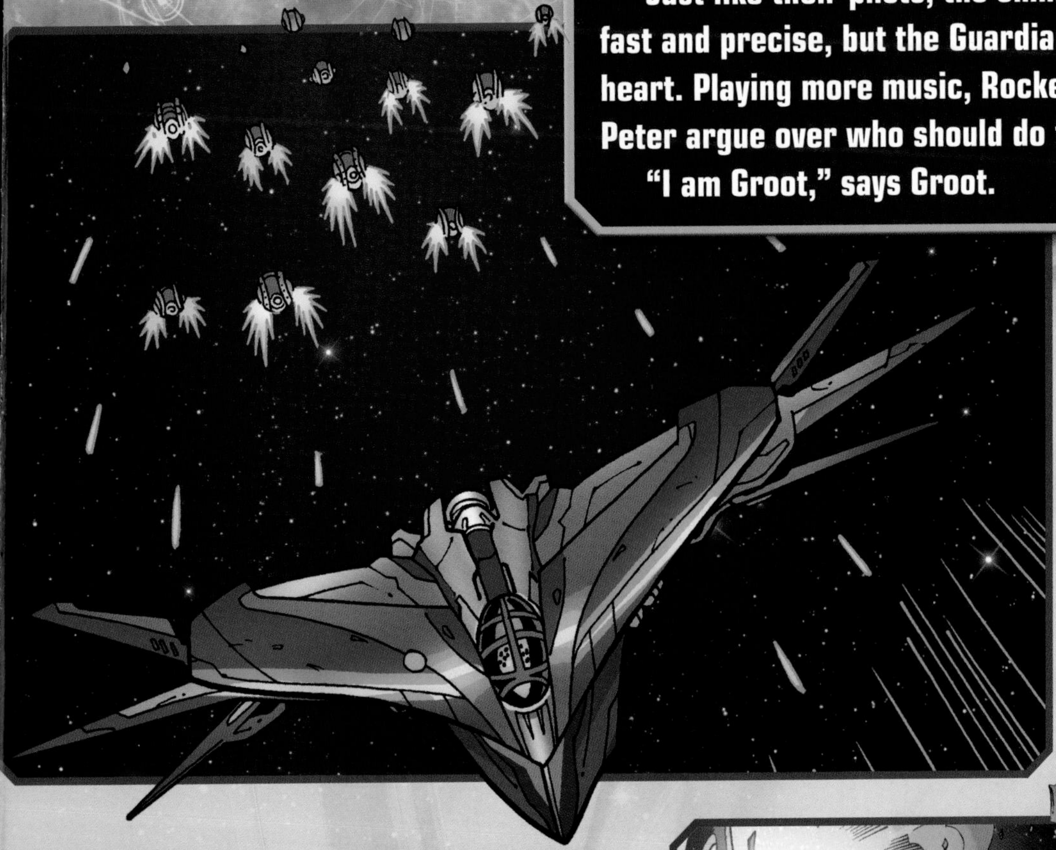

Peter weaves the vessel through the incoming fire as Rocket unleashes hits of his own. "Nailed ya!" Rocket cheers as one of the pods explodes.

"I am Groot!" his friend yells in agreement.

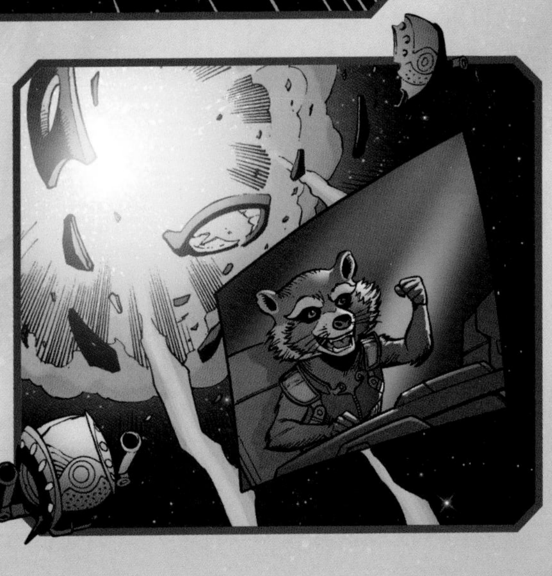

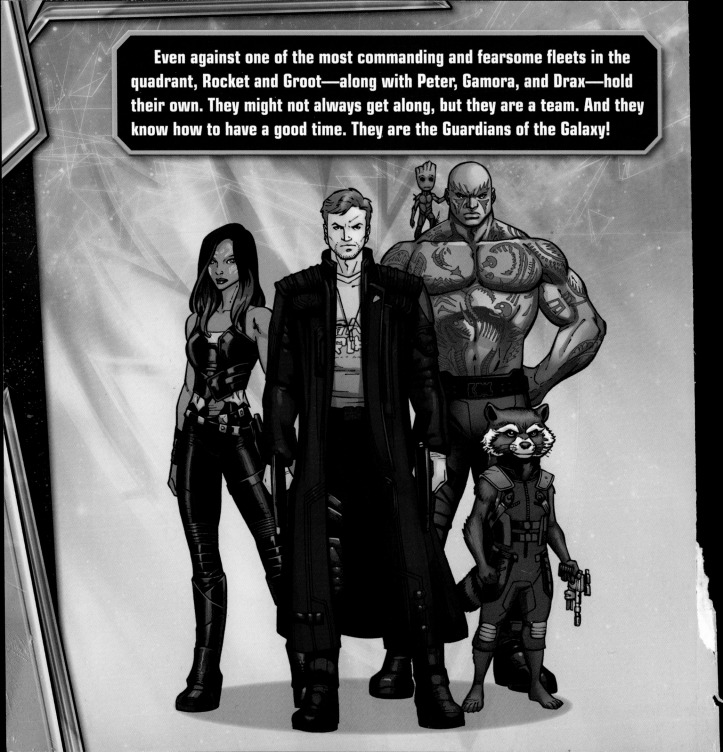

Even against one of the most commanding and fearsome fleets in the quadrant, Rocket and Groot—along with Peter, Gamora, and Drax—hold their own. They might not always get along, but they are a team. And they know how to have a good time. They are the Guardians of the Galaxy!